❖ WALTER HILL ❖
THE COWBOY ILIAD

A COMPANION BOOKLET
TO THE SPOKEN WORD ALBUM

⤞WALTER HILL⤝
THE COWBOY ILIAD

A COMPANION BOOKLET
TO THE SPOKEN WORD ALBUM

MARMONT LANE
BOOKS

MARMONT LANE
BOOKS

The Cowboy Iliad

For information address Marmont Lane Books
139 South Beverly Drive Suite 318
Beverly Hills, CA USA 90212

marmontlane.com

Second Printing

Publisher: Bobby Woods/Marmont Lane Books

Design: ♡✕☕≡⚡

Cover Painting: *A Dash For The Timber* by Frederic Remington

ISBN 13: 978-0-9998527-6-7
Library of Congress Control Number: 2019933116

Westerns Directed By Walter Hill

The Long Riders

Geronimo: An American Legend

Wild Bill

Deadwood

Broken Trail

For

The Cowboy On The Porch

WALTER HILL
THE COWBOY ILIAD

A COMPANION BOOKLET
TO THE SPOKEN WORD ALBUM

MARMONT LANE
BOOKS

"When a legend becomes a fact,

print the legend."

⚹ Contents ⚹

⁂ **1** ⁂

The Killing Of William Bailey

EWTON, KANSAS —— 1871.

BACK THEN, NEWTON WAS LIKE ABILENE,
DODGE OR WICHITA ——
A RAILROAD TOWN AND CATTLE TOWN STUCK
AT THE FAR END OF THE CHISOLM TRAIL...

MOST WAYS, THESE PLACES WERE ABOUT
THE SAME.

LOOSE MONEY.

NOT MUCH LAW AND ORDER.

EVERYBODY WEARING A GUN.

EVERYBODY DRINKING WHISKY...

THE TROUBLE BEGAN ON THE AFTERNOON
OF AUGUST 11TH, WITH AN ARGUMENT AND
A FIST FIGHT ——

BETWEEN WILLIAM BAILEY, A PROFESSIONAL
GAMBLER...
AND MIKE MCCLUSKEY, A RAILROAD YARD
FOREMAN AND SECURITY MAN.

NEEDLESS TO SAY, BOTH MEN WERE DRUNK...

THE FIGHT TOOK PLACE IN THE RED FRONT
SALOON ABOUT FOUR IN THE AFTERNOON.

MCCLUSKEY WAS A BIG MAN, AND HE KNOCKED
BAILEY THROUGH THE SALOON DOORS AND
OUT INTO THE STREET.
BAILEY GOT TO HIS FEET AND WENT FOR HIS
PISTOL —— MCCLUSKEY DID THE SAME.

A STAREDOWN FOLLOWED.

THEN MCCLUSKEY FIRED TWO SHOTS...
THE SECOND ONE HIT BAILEY IN THE GUT.
BAILEY DIED THE FOLLOWING DAY.
EVEN THOUGH BAILEY HADN'T FIRED HIS GUN,
MCCLUSKEY CLAIMED SELF-DEFENSE...

ONE MORE ITEM WAS TO BEAR HEAVILY ON
THE SITUATION:

THE DEAD MAN WAS FROM TEXAS.

AND TWO DAYS AFTER THE SHOOTING, A HERD
OF OVER A THOUSAND TEXAS CATTLE ARRIVED
IN NEWTON.

SEVERAL OF THE WRANGLERS WHO HAD
DRIVEN THE HERD WERE FRIENDS OF BAILEY
——

THERE WAS TALK OF REVENGE.

———•◦•———

⚔ 2 ⚔

The Shootout
At Perry Tuttle's Dance Hall

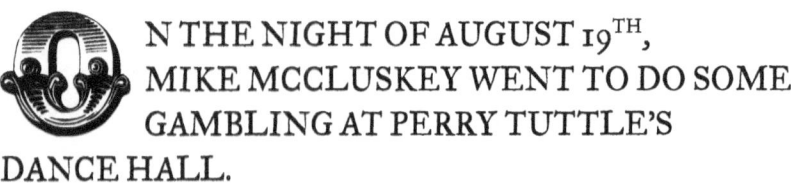N THE NIGHT OF AUGUST 19TH, MIKE MCCLUSKEY WENT TO DO SOME GAMBLING AT PERRY TUTTLE'S DANCE HALL.

HE WAS ACCOMPANIED BY ANOTHER RAILROAD MAN... A FRIEND NAMED MARTIN.
JIM MARTIN.

MCCLUSKEY SAT IN ON A POKER GAME FOR ABOUT AN HOUR, THEN MOVED ON TO THE FARO TABLE.

AROUND THAT TIME, THREE OF THE NEWLY ARRIVED TEXAS COWBOYS ENTERED THE CROWDED DANCE HALL.

THEY WERE:
BILLY GARRETT. HENRY KEARNES. AND JIM WILKERSON.

MAYBE TEN MINUTES LATER,
HUGH ANDERSON ARRIVED.

ANDERSON WAS ANOTHER TEXAN,
A COWHAND, AND, IT TURNED OUT, ANOTHER
GOOD FRIEND OF WILLIAM BAILEY.

HUGH ANDERSON JOINED HIS THREE FRIENDS
AT THE LONG BAR, ORDERED A WHISKY OF
HIS OWN...
HE WANTED A DOUBLE —
AND HE GOT IT.

HUGH ANDERSON WAS TWENTY-TWO YEARS OLD.

ALL SMILES, THE TEXANS CLINKED GLASSES,
SIPPED THEIR WHISKY...
MIKE MCCLUSKEY JUST KEPT PLAYING FARO...
JIM MARTIN KEPT AN EYE OUT, WATCHING THE
TEXANS...

AN OUT OF TUNE PIANO KEPT PLAYING.

HUGH ANDERSON FINISHED HIS DRINK,
THEN WALKED TO THE FARO TABLE ——

HE IMMEDIATELY CALLED MCCLUSKEY
A COWARD.

SAID HE WAS GOING TO KILL HIM.

ANDERSON'S SLUG GOT MCCLUSKEY IN
THE NECK.

THE IMPACT FROM THE BULLET SENT
MCCLUSKEY TO THE FLOOR.

JIM MARTIN WAS NOW WRESTLING WITH
ANDERSON ——

MCCLUSKEY GOT HIS PISTOL OUT, TRIED TO
SHOOT ANDERSON, BUT HIS GUN MISFIRED.

ANDERSON BROKE FREE, STOOD OVER
MCCLUSKEY — KICKED HIM TWICE —
THEN, AS THE FALLEN MAN TRIED TO CRAWL
AWAY — SHOT MCCLUSKEY,
THREE TIMES IN THE BACK.

AT THE SAME TIME, ON THE OTHER SIDE OF
THE ROOM:

GARRETT, KEARNES AND WILKERSON ALL
BEGAN BLASTING AWAY ——

THEIR VOLLEY OF GUNFIRE HIT JIM MARTIN
SEVERAL TIMES...
ALSO HITTING MCCLUSKEY IN THE LEG AND
HIP — THEN ONE MORE, DEEP IN THE LUNG.

JIM MARTIN RAN OUT OF THE DANCE HALL,
GOT TO THE MIDDLE OF THE STREET,
FELL NOSE-DOWN IN THE DIRT... AND DIED.

———

BACK INSIDE TUTTLE'S, THERE WAS A HELLISH
MIX OF SCATTERED PATRONS, SMOKE, BLOOD,
SCREAMING AND DYING MEN...
AND A NEW SHOOTER WAS IN THE ROOM.

A FRIEND OF MCCLUSKEY.

A MAN WHO DIDN'T LIKE TEXANS.

THIS WAS JAMES RILEY.

IF THAT WAS HIS REAL NAME.

NO ONE KNEW WHERE HE CAME FROM.

HE WAS SAID TO BE JUST PAST HIS EIGHTEENTH
BIRTHDAY. HE WAS SAID TO BE IN TROUBLE
WITH THE LAW. HE WAS ALSO SAID TO BE DYING
OF TUBERCULOSIS.

BUT HE WAS A FRIEND OF MCCLUSKEY.
AND HE STOOD BY HIS FRIEND.

HE WORE TWO GUNS.
HE KNEW HOW TO USE THEM.

HE KILLED GARRETT, KEARNES AND ONE OF
THE PATRONS WHO DREW HIS PISTOL.

IN THE MIX OF BLAZING GUNFIRE, RILEY
BADLY WOUNDED HUGH ANDERSON AND
JIM WILKERSON, ALONG WITH ANOTHER
BYSTANDER——

AN UNLUCKY FELLOW WHO JUST GOT IN
THE WAY...

RILEY FINISHED THE GUNFIGHT WITH BOTH
PISTOLS EMPTY——
AND ALL OF HIS OPPONENTS ON THE FLOOR.

THINKING HIS FRIEND MCCLUSKEY WAS DEAD,
RILEY WALKED OUT OF PERRY TUTTLE'S DANCE
HALL, SADDLED A HORSE AND LEFT TOWN
WITHIN THE HOUR.

AND WITH THAT, JAMES RILEY DISAPPEARED.

SOME BELIEVE HE DIED FROM CONSUMPTION
SOON AFTER ——
AND PROBABLY DIED UNDER AN ASSUMED NAME.
OTHERS SAID JAMES RILEY WAS ALREADY AN
ASSUMED NAME.

ONLY ONE THING IS CERTAIN:
HE VANISHED INTO THE NIGHT...

AND WAS NEVER HEARD FROM AGAIN.

IT TURNED OUT MCCLUSKEY WAS STILL
BREATHING ——

THEY LUGGED HIM OVER TO A HOTEL ROOM
ACROSS THE STREET.

BUT HIS CONDITION WAS HOPELESS.

MIKE MCCLUSKEY FINALLY DIED THE FOLLOWING MORNING.

DIED HARD.

HIS SCREAMS OF AGONY COULD BE HEARD ALL THE WAY DOWN TO THE CATTLE PENS JUST OUTSIDE OF TOWN...

⚒ 3 ⚒

And What Of Hugh Anderson?

ND WHAT OF HUGH ANDERSON?

HUGH ANDERSON, WHO HAILED FROM
WACO AND WAS SAID TO BE FRIENDLY WITH
NOTORIOUS JOHN WESLEY HARDIN...

HUGH ANDERSON, WHO WAS INFURIATED BY
THE SHOOTING OF GAMBLER AND FRIEND,
WILLIAM BAILEY...

HUGH ANDERSON, WHO HAD ENDEAVORED TO
DEFEND THE HONOR OF TEXAS AND TEXANS...

HUGH ANDERSON, WHO HAD FIRED THE
FIRST SHOT...

AND, FOR ALL HIS TROUBLE, BEEN PAID OFF IN
SPADES BY MR. JAMES RILEY.

HUGH ANDERSON ENDED THE EVENING BEING
BADLY SHOT IN BOTH LEGS, TAKING ANOTHER
BULLET THROUGH ONE OF HIS HIPS AND
ANOTHER HIGH IN THE CHEST, SMASHING HIS
COLLARBONE.

REMORSELESS,
JAMES RILEY LEFT HIM FOR DEAD.

———•—•———

LATER, AS ALL THE BODIES WERE BEING
CARRIED OUT...

IT GOT NOTICED THAT HUGH ANDERSON WAS
STILL BREATHING...
HE GOT SOME MEDICAL CARE...
THEY DUG THE BULLETS OUT...
PUMPED HIM FULL OF WHISKY.
SEVERAL OF THE TEXAS COWBOYS WATCHED
OVER HIM — DAY AND NIGHT.

A WEEK WENT BY...
NO INFECTION SET IN.
SOMEHOW, HUGH ANDERSON GOT BETTER.
HE STARTED TO GET AROUND ON CRUTCHES.

IT WAS SAID A WARRANT WOULD SOON BE ISSUED
FOR THE KILLING OF MIKE MCCLUSKEY.

SO HUGH ANDERSON, IN THE DEAD OF NIGHT,
LEFT KANSAS BY TRAIN.

MADE HIS WAY BACK HOME TO TEXAS...
THEN SETTLED IN THE INDIAN TERRITORY, TO
HIDE OUT AND RECOVER FROM HIS WOUNDS.

AND HUGH ANDERSON MANAGED TO STAY OUT OF
SIGHT FOR THE NEXT TWO YEARS...

BUT ONE THING WAS SURE,
HUGH ANDERSON WAS A MARKED MAN.

⁕ 4 ⁕

The Casualties

F ONE COUNTS WILLIAM BAILEY FROM THE WEEK BEFORE ——

THE FIGHT THAT NIGHT IN PERRY TUTTLE'S DANCE HALL HAD LEFT SIX DEAD...
THREE MORE SEVERELY WOUNDED...
TWO OF THEM CRIPPLED FOR LIFE...

THIS IS ALL TRUE. YOU CAN LOOK IT UP.

BUT THERE WAS MORE TO COME ——

IT WOULD TAKE A WHILE, BUT THE ANDERSON/MCCLUSKEY STORY WOULDN'T END WITHOUT A PROPER CONCLUSION.

MORE BLOOD.

AND MORE REVENGE.

⚹ 5 ⚹

The Duel At Medicine Lodge

N THE NEXT PART OF OUR STORY THE FACTS ARE NOT AS CERTAIN.

THIS MUCH WE KNOW:

MIKE MCCLUSKEY HAD A BROTHER.
HE WAS A YEAR OLDER, AND WENT BY THE
NAME OF ARTHUR ——
AND ARTHUR MCCLUSKEY WAS NOT
RECONCILED TO BROTHER MIKE'S DEATH.
AND HE WASN'T RECONCILED TO THE IDEA
THAT HUGH ANDERSON HAD ESCAPED
PROPER RETRIBUTION.

ARTHUR MCCLUSKEY, LIKE HIS DEAD BROTHER,
WAS A BIG FELLOW —
AND GOOD WITH BOTH FIST AND PISTOL.
IT TOOK TWO YEARS FOR ARTHUR MCCLUSKEY
TO FIND HUGH ANDERSON —

AND HE DID.

ON JULY 23, 1873, *THE NEW YORK WORLD* PUBLISHED A PAGE ONE STORY.

THE HEADLINE READ:

> *MEETING OF THE DESPERADOES HUGH ANDERSON OF TEXAS AND ARTHUR MCCLUSKEY OF KANSAS.*

THE NEWSPAPER ARTICLE THEN TOLD THE FOLLOWING TALE, QUOTE:

> *ONE OF THE MOST FEROCIOUS DUELS EVER FOUGHT.*
>
> *BOTH DESPERADOES WELL-KNOWN FOR THEIR RECKLESSNESS OF LIFE.*
>
> *IT OCCURRED ON JULY 4, IN INDIAN TERRITORY.*
>
> *BY THE TERMS AGREED UPON, THE ANTAGONISTS WERE TO FIGHT TO THE*

DEATH —— WITH PISTOLS AND BOWIE KNIVES.

THE TWO DUELISTS TO BE PLACED BACK-TO-BACK AT AN INTERVAL OF TWENTY PACES...

BOTH MEN TO WHEEL AND FIRE AT A GIVEN SIGNAL.

AND AFTER THE FIRST SHOTS, CONDUCT THE FIGHT AS EACH MAN SHOULD DEEM TO BEST PERSONAL ADVANTAGE.

❉ 6 ❉

Awaiting The Signal

THE SPOT SELECTED FOR THE ENCOUNTER WAS ON THE OPEN PRAIRIE, SEVERAL HUNDRED YARDS DISTANT FROM HARDING'S TRADING POST AT THE EDGE OF TOWN.

ABOUT 70 LOCALS SHOWED UP TO WATCH — BETS WERE MADE...
MOST FAVORED MCCLUSKEY BECAUSE HE WAS THE CHALLENGER, THE REVENGER AND THE BIGGER MAN SHOULD IT COME DOWN TO HAND-TO-HAND COMBAT...

IT WAS EARLY EVENING. ALMOST SUNSET.

LITTLE TIME WAS WASTED IN PRELIMINARIES.

TWENTY PACES WERE STEPPED OFF.

THE SPECTATORS DREW BACK TO WHAT WAS CONSIDERED A SAFE DISTANCE.

BOTH MEN STOOD ON THEIR MARKS ——

THEIR BACKS TO EACH OTHER, LIKE STATUES
LOOMING AGAINST THE FADING LIGHT ——
BOTH AWAITING THE SIGNAL...

———

MCCLUSKEY WAS THE FIRST TO FIRE.

RAPIDLY FOLLOWED BY ANDERSON'S
FIRST SHOT —

THEN A MOMENTARY PAUSE.

ANDERSON HAD A DEEP FURROW ON THE
CHEEK, DRAWING IMMEDIATE BLOOD.

MCCLUSKEY REMAINED STANDING,
APPEARING UNHARMED.

BUT THIS WAS NOT THE CASE.

HE JERKED WITH A SUDDEN SPASM,
THEN LEVELED HIS PISTOL AND FIRED AGAIN.

THIS TIME HIS BULLET BROKE ANDERSON'S
LEFT ARM.

THE TEXAN SCREAMED, FELL TO ONE KNEE,
RETURNED FIRE...

THIS TIME WITH WICKED EFFECT.

ONE OF ANDERSON'S BULLETS HAD TORN
THROUGH MCCLUSKEY'S FACE...
RIPPING AWAY PART OF THE JAWBONE, TAKING
SEVERAL TEETH, AND SOME OF MCCLUSKEY'S
TONGUE.

SOMEHOW, MCCLUSKEY STAGGERED FORWARD
A FEW STEPS, TRIED TO STEADY HIMSELF...
HIS MOUTH HANGING OPEN.
BLOOD POURING IN TORRENTS...

ANDERSON FIRED ANOTHER SHOT, WHICH HIT
AND BROKE MCCLUSKEY'S SHOULDER.

ANDERSON FIRED ONE MORE TIME —— HIS
LAST BULLET —— WHICH HIT MCCLUSKEY IN
THE PIT OF THE STOMACH.

BUT MCCLUSKEY STILL HAD A CLOSE HOLD ON
HIS PISTOL.

HE AIMED WITH GREAT EFFORT...

ANDERSON WAS HIT JUST BELOW THE
BELLY BUTTON.

HE BEGAN WRITHING AND TWISTING ON THE
GROUND IN UNCONTROLLABLE CONTORTIONS.

ANDERSON, LIKE MCCLUSKEY,
WAS NOW A FAST DYING MAN.

⚜ 7 ⚜

The Dying And The Dead

HE FINALE WAS NOW AT HAND.

THE CURTAIN ALMOST READY TO DROP.

MCCLUSKEY SOMEHOW DREW HIS FOOT-LONG BOWIE KNIFE AND BEGAN CRAWLING TOWARD ANDERSON.

BOTH MEN HAD DROPPED THEIR EMPTY REVOLVERS.

ANDERSON — SEEING THE BLOOD-COVERED MCCLUSKEY CRAWLING TOWARD HIM — WAS ABLE TO COME UP WITH HIS OWN BLADE...

AS MCCLUSKEY CRAWLED WITHIN REACH, ANDERSON CAUGHT HIM IN THE THROAT — CUTTING MUSCLE, TENDONS, VEINS...

A DYING ANDERSON FELL FORWARD...

AND AS MCCLUSKEY, GASPING, WENT TO MEET
HIS MAKER,
HE STABBED ANDERSON TWICE IN THE BACK —

THEN FELL DEAD
ACROSS HIS OPPONENTS BODY.

⚜ 8 ⚜

No Gambling

HERE WAS NO GAMBLING IN MEDICINE LODGE THAT NIGHT.

MOST FOLKS FIGURED THERE WAS PLENTY ENOUGH EXCITEMENT JUST DISCUSSING THE RECENT SPECTACLE.

THE MANGLED CORPSES OF THE TWO DUELISTS LAY IN REPOSE ON THE TRADING POST'S WOODEN PORCH.

———•◦•———

ON THAT PARTICULAR NIGHT, THE MOON ROSE AT ABOUT ELEVEN O'CLOCK...

THE BODIES OF HUGH ANDERSON AND ARTHUR MCCLUSKEY WERE CARRIED OUT ONTO

THE PRAIRIE.

NO FUNERAL CEREMONIES WERE PERFORMED.

BUT, OUT OF RESPECT,
THEY WERE BURIED DEEP —

NO ONE PRESENT WANTED THE TWO BRAVE
MEN TO BE EATEN BY THE WOLVES OR
COYOTES.

❊ 9 ❊

Whisky & Pistols

KAY. END OF STORY.

NOW, WHAT'S IT ALL ABOUT?
WHAT, IF ANY, LESSONS ARE TO BE DRAWN?

OBVIOUSLY, WE CAN SAY, 'WHISKY AND PISTOLS
ARE A BAD MIX.'

AND THAT ATTEMPTS FOR PERSONAL JUSTICE
ARE OFTEN JUST AN EXCUSE FOR VIOLENCE...

THOSE ARE EASY JUDGMENTS.

BUT THE DARK SIDE WITHIN US ALL
HAS ITS OWN LOGIC —

SURE...

WE REACH FOR THE STARS.

AND SOMETIMES, TRUTH BE TOLD,
WE REACH FOR THE BULLET, OR THE BLADE.

———·•·———

⚹ 10 ⚹

Big Lies

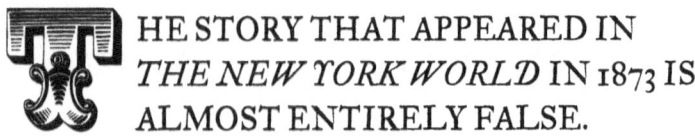HE STORY THAT APPEARED IN
THE NEW YORK WORLD IN 1873 IS
ALMOST ENTIRELY FALSE.

NONE OF THE SEVENTY WITNESSES
WERE EVER FOUND.
NOR WERE THERE CORROBORATING ACCOUNTS
BY ANY OFFICIAL CONTEMPORARY SOURCES. NOR
WAS THERE A TOWN OR VILLAGE IN THE INDIAN
NATION CALLED 'MEDICINE LODGE.'

AND THE NEWSPAPERS IN KANSAS HAD
IMMEDIATELY LABELED *THE NEW YORK
WORLD'S* ACCOUNT OF THE DUEL:

A COMPLETE LIE.

FURTHER RESEARCH HAS SHOWN THAT HUGH
ANDERSON WAS ALIVE UNTIL THE YEAR 1914,
WHEN HE WAS KILLED BY LIGHTNING.
HE WAS 62 YEARS OLD.

DESPITE ALL THIS, OVER THE DECADES, THE STORY OF THE DUEL AT MEDICINE LODGE GAINED CONSIDERABLE CREDIBILITY.

BOTH CASUAL AND SERIOUS HISTORIANS WROTE IT UP AS A NEAR-IDEAL EXAMPLE OF FRONTIER JUSTICE AND REVENGE.

THE DUEL THAT NEVER HAPPENED WAS CONSCIOUSLY, OR UNCONSCIOUSLY, UNDERSTOOD TO BE A PERFECT COMPLIMENT TO THE SHOOTOUT IN PERRY TUTTLE'S DANCE HALL.

AS A POET SAID, 'SOMETIMES THE MYTH BECOMES THE GREATER TRUTH.'

AND ANOTHER POET SAID, 'WHEN A LEGEND BECOMES A FACT, PRINT THE LEGEND.'

⊰ 11 ⊱

Epilogue

O HERE WE HAVE IT.

A PRIME EXAMPLE OF AMERICAN GOTHIC...
SET ON THE VAST PRAIRIES OF THE WILDERNESS.

IT ALL SPEAKS OF THE OLD REPUBLIC —
AND THE WEST, THE *HARD* WEST:
THE ORDEALS OF COMBAT THAT DEFINE HONOR,
THE STRICT ADHERENCE TO TRIBAL CODES, YET,
SIMULTANEOUSLY, BEHAVIOR OF RECKLESS
ABANDON...

WITH DEATH AS A COMPANION TO CHANCES
TAKEN, RISKS ACCEPTED, CHALLENGES MET; AND,
BY GOD, MOST OF IT DONE WITH GRIT, AND A TEAR,
AND A SONG, AND A SMILE.

OR SO GOES THE LEGEND.

BUT STILL...
MAYBE IT'S NOT JUST A TRUE ANECDOTE.
FOLLOWED BY A LURID FALSEHOOD.

MAYBE IT'S DEEPER...

WAY BEYOND COWBOYS AND SALOONS,
AND PISTOLS, AND TEXANS AND WHISKY,
AND MYSTERIOUS STRANGERS, AND SO MANY
OF OUR DARK PLACES.

MAYBE SEE IT THIS WAY:
MAYBE IT GOES *ALL THE WAY BACK* —

THE FIRST STORIES TOLD AROUND CAMPFIRES...
OLD TESTAMENT...
OR HOMER IN MINIATURE...

THE ILIAD WRIT SMALL...

IT KIND OF TRACKS THAT WAY ——

BEGINNING WITH A WRONGFUL ACT...
THEN WOUNDED PRIDE...
MOVING TO A BATTLE ROYAL...

ENDING WITH A BLOOD AND THUNDER
RE-ENACTMENT OF HECTOR AND ACHILLES.

NOT BEFORE THE WALLS OF TROY ——
BUT WITHIN THE DARK CONFINES OF MR. PERRY
TUTTLE'S DANCE HALL.

OR DO WE CLAIM TOO MUCH?

ANOTHER CASE CAN BE MADE:

JUST DUMB DRUNKEN COWBOYS, SLUGGING
AND SHOOTING IT OUT... OVER MISBEHAVIOR BY
OTHER DUMB DRUNKEN COWBOYS...

AND FOR US TO INVEST THEIR ACTIONS
WITH IDEAS OF HEROISM, NOSTALGIA, AND
PRIMITIVE NOBILITY —— EVEN IN THE POETIC
SENSE —— IS FAR MORE THAN THE FREIGHT
WILL BEAR.

OR IS IT?

THIS SINGER OF TALES DETECTS THE OLDEST
OF STORIES...
AND THE OLD HARD RELIGION OF COURAGE.
AND THE DEEPEST MELANCHOLY OF
LOST HORIZONS.

WHAT SAY YOU, NOBLE LISTENER?
WHAT SAY YOU?

END.

⸺•⸺

W.H.

MARCH — 2019

⚜ Acknowledgements ⚜

There would be no Cowboy Iliad without the skill and dedication of Bobby Woods, the musicians of Les Deux Love Orchestra, the efforts of Hope Anita Smith, Phil Norden, and the patience of my dear wife Hildy.

The Harvey County Historical Museum in Newton, Kansas supplied valuable information in my attempt to sort out disputed events from nearly 150 years ago.

I'd also like to thank Christopher Logue, Sam Peckinpah, and Sam Shepard, absent friends who —— without their knowledge —— contributed greatly in various ways.

Finally, to Greil Marcus, whose *The Old, Weird America* sent me along this path, and from whom I borrowed a phrase in the text. We take what we must.

W.H.

⚹ About The Author ⚹

Walter Hill was born in Long Beach, California. He has written and directed films since the early 1970's.

For his work in Westerns he has won two Outstanding Directorial Achievement Awards [DGA], two Emmys [Academy of Television Arts and Sciences], two Golden Boot Awards [MPTF], and two Western Heritage Wrangler Awards [National Cowboy Hall of Fame].

FOR THEIR ASSISTANCE IN THE MAKING OF THIS COMPANION BOOKLET,
MARMONT LANE BOOKS WOULD LIKE TO THANK
HOPE ANITA SMITH, TOM ANDRE, ANDREW GOLOMB, CHARLIE HAYGOOD,
CARMINE'S RESTAURANT, JORGE MENDOZA, CYNTHIA BELL, ELLEN BASKIN,

AND LISA CLANCY — WHO PAID FOR THE GUN.

Marmont Lane

BOOKS

MARMONTLANE.COM